DUSTY

DUSTY

BY
NOLA LANGNER

Xerox Education Publications ✤ Middletown, Connecticut

This book is for
Arnie, Ruth, Hilary,
Sandy, and Tony
and with special thanks
to Saroya.

On Monday night
the wind was blowing,

and Dusty came to my door.

She was hungry.

But she didn't come in.

She sat outside

and listened to the wind.

Mama said she was wild

and lived outside.

Monday, Dusty hated water.

She loved milk and tuna fish.

After she ate,

she went into the dark woods.

The trees were big and black.

There was no moon.

On Tuesday night
it was raining hard.
Dusty was under the porch.
I opened the door,
and she came in.
She was hungry again.
Tuesday night,
Dusty hated tuna fish.
She loved milk
and cold spaghetti
and tomato sauce.

When she had eaten half of everything,
she went to the door
and made sure
it was still open.

Then she walked
out on the porch
and cleaned herself off.
After that,
she came back in
and finished.
I called to her when
she left.

But all I heard

was the rain.

At sunset on Wednesday
I heard Dusty.
I let her in.
I left the door open for her.
This time
she hated cold spaghetti
and tomato sauce.
She loved milk with
an egg mixed in it.

When she had eaten
half of everything,
she went to the door and
made sure
it was still open.
Then she walked outside
and cleaned herself off.
She let me pet her,
out there.

When she came back in,
to finish eating,
she let me pick her up.

It was dark when she left.

I knew she wouldn't stay.

When I went to bed
on Thursday,
I thought she
wouldn't come.
But she did.

For such a large cat,

she had a very small meow.

She still loved milk and eggs,
but I also had to give her
cottage cheese, tiny green peas,
and some small pieces of chicken
without the skin.
Dusty ate half of everything.

Then she sat on my lap
and let me pet her.
She purred.
After she finished eating,
she walked in and out
of the door.
I thought maybe she would stay.
But she left.

That night she turned and looked

back at me ·

when I said good-night.

Early Friday morning
there was Dusty.
She was walking very slowly.

She had a cut on her paw.
Mama said she had
a fight with an animal.
She took some milk and egg,
some cottage cheese,
but she wouldn't touch
peas or chicken.
That morning
she loved canned corn.
I shut the door.
Dusty didn't mind.

Halfway through her meal,
she fell asleep.
She stayed asleep all day.
Purred and slept.
Slept and purred.
Friday night
she felt much better.

I opened the door.
I knew she wanted
to go outside.
She rubbed against my leg
before she left.

I waited all day Saturday,

but no Dusty.

I looked everywhere outside.

A big dog was barking.

I thought of Dusty all alone.

I called to her.

But she didn't come.

After supper

I looked out the door.

She wasn't there.

I woke up in the night.
There was a full moon.
Suddenly I saw her.

She was sitting
very quietly
under the bird feeder,
waiting for birds.

I called to her.
She swished her tail,
but she didn't come in.

It was raining
on Sunday.
Dusty didn't return
until afternoon,
when the sun came out.
She was very hungry.

She meowed and purred while
I fixed her milk and egg.

She was so hungry

that I got out everything.

The tuna fish,

the cold spaghetti and tomato sauce,

the cottage cheese,

the tiny peas,

the chicken,

and the canned corn.

She ate it all.

She didn't even stop

halfway through.

Dusty stayed all summer.

During the day

she slept

on the cool side of the living room.

When the sun set,
she sat outside
in the tall grass,
waiting for birds.
Some nights,
she slept on the chair
in my room.
She didn't wake up
when I got up.
She woke up
when she was ready.
But most nights,
she stayed outside.

Then it got to be fall.
The leaves on the oak tree
turned brown.
The leaves
on the maple tree
were bright red.

That was when
Dusty went away.

It was a hot night
in September.
The moon was shining,
and there were fireflies.
She went out.
But she never came back.
Mama says
it was just her time to go.

We never said good-bye.
But I'll bet she
still remembers me.
Because Dusty and me,
we were friends.

Nola Langner is a graduate of Bennington College and has studied at the Yale Summer School of Fine Arts and Parsons School of Design. She began her career as an artist doing illustrations for television and advertising and has since illustrated and written more than thirty books. *Scram Kid* for which she did the drawings received the Boston *Globe* Horn Book Award for best illustration in 1975.

Mrs. Langner makes her home in New York City with her husband, Thomas, a professor of Sociology at Columbia University, their five children, and seven Siamese cats.